u y

D0314274

For my grandchildren

First published in Great Britain in 2009 by
Piccadilly Press Ltd, 5 Castle Road, London NW1 8PR
www.piccadillypress.co.uk

Text and illustration copyright © Tony Maddox, 2009

All rights reserved. No part of this publication may be reproduced,
stored in a retrieval system, or transmitted, in any form or by any
means, electronic, mechanical, photocopying or otherwise, without
prior permission of the copyright owner.

The right of Tony Maddox to be recognised as Author and
Illustrator of this work has been asserted by him in accordance
with the Copyright, Designs and Patents Act 1988.

Designed by Simon Davis
Printed and bound in China by WKT
Colour reproduction by Dot Gradations

ISBN: 978 1 84812 016 7 (hardback)
978 1 84812 015 0 (paperback)

1 3 5 7 9 10 8 6 4 2

# Little Croc
## and Whale

**WARWICKSHIRE LIBRARY & INFORMATION SERVICE**

| 013255981 3 | |
|---|---|
| £5.99 | 10-Jul-2009 |
| | |

# Tony Maddox

Piccadilly Press • London

Little Croc was bored with
swimming in the lake.
Wouldn't it be fun, he thought,
to swim in the rapids, where the river
runs fast and deep?

'The rapids are too dangerous for
a small crocodile,' warned Bird.
But Little Croc didn't listen.

In he jumped and the fast-flowing
water carried him along.
'This is fun!' he cried.
'Watch out for the waterfall!' shouted Bird
... but it was too late!

Together,

they shot over the

top of the waterfall.

Bird flew up into the air

but Little Croc plunged

into the river below

and was swept out to

the big, wide ocean.

Little Croc tried to swim,
but the waves were too strong.

'Save me, Bird!' he cried . . .

. . . but there was nothing Bird could do!

Suddenly,
Little Croc felt
himself being lifted
out of the water . . .

higher and higher . . .

He was on
the back of a
GIANT
WHALE!

'Hold tight,' said Whale.
'I'll soon have you
back on dry land.'

Little Croc thanked Whale for saving him.
He and Bird had just set off on their long journey home,
when they heard a shout.

'HELP!'

It was Whale!

He was stuck on a sandbank.

Little Croc and Bird
did their best to push
Whale back into the
sea . . . but he was
much too heavy!

The sun was getting
hotter and hotter.
'We need help!'
gasped
Little Croc.

There was no time to lose.
Little Croc splashed water over Whale
to keep him cool

. . . and Bird flew back into the jungle as fast as he could. 'Quick!' he called to the animals. 'We need your help!'

Trumpeting loudly, the elephants led
the other animals down to the
beach to try to save Whale.

Together, they pushed and they pulled,
they pulled and they pushed.

But they couldn't move Whale. He was well and truly stuck!

Then the elephants had a very good idea. They all took a deep breath, puffed up their cheeks and *BLEW*
and *BLEW*
and *BLEW*
on the sea around Whale

. . . until they made a huge wave that washed
Whale off the sandbank and into the sea.
'Hooray!' they all cried.

With a grateful wave of his flipper
and a flick of his tail, Whale headed
out to the open sea.

The next day, Little Croc and Bird were safely back in the lake.

'It's not so bad here, really,' said Little Croc, 'but I can't

help wondering where the other part of the river goes.'

Bird gave a loud groan.

'I'm only joking!' laughed Little Croc.

Or was he?